THE CLOCKMAKER WHO TRAVELLED THROUGH TIME

TAHIR SHAH

ANCA CHELARU

THE CLOCKMAKER WHO TRAVELLED THROUGH TIME

A Teaching Story

TAHIR SHAH

ANCA CHELARU

MMXXIV

Secretum Mundi Publishing Ltd
124 City Road
London
EC1V 2NX
United Kingdom

www.secretum-mundi.com
info@secretum-mundi.com

First published by Secretum Mundi Publishing Ltd, 2024
A version of this story originally appeared in *Scorpion Soup* by Tahir Shah, 2013

THE CLOCKMAKER WHO TRAVELLED THROUGH TIME

Artwork drawn by Anca Chelaru

A CIP catalogue record for this title is available from the British Library.

ISBN 978-1-915876-09-6

VERSION 17012024

Visit the author's website:
Tahirshah.com

Feed your neighbours before you feed yourself.

Moroccan saying

Teaching Stories

WHEN I WAS small, I was told stories from morning till night.

I was told stories about genies and witches and about great birds that could carry away elephants on their wings... and stories about distant kingdoms and magical lands ruled by warrior kings.

I was told stories of good and bad... stories of hope and others of despair.

I was even told stories about stories.

And all the while, I listened, amazed.

The more I listened, the more my mind worked... and the more I came to understand that these stories had a power about them, a secret lifeblood all of their own.

They were magical instruments, machineries that could alter states of mind and change the way we think.

But most importantly of all, stories can teach us, without us realizing that they are doing so at all.

Part of the default programming of man, stories are within us all.

Born into us, they make us who we are – they make us human.

Since earliest childhood, I have feasted on stories as a way of learning about the world, and learning about myself. They have been my dictionary and my encyclopaedia, my classroom, my guide, and my very best friend.

To descend down through the layers of stories is to be reborn, into a dominion of fantasy – one touched by real magic.

Pre-eminent within the great treasuries of tales, it is teaching stories like this one that have shown me the path to follow beyond the next horizon, and have made me the man I am.

Tahir Shah

There was once a clockmaker whose work was patronized by the rich, and whose expertise was so excellent that word of his skill reached the ears of the sultan himself.

Obsessed with mechanical devices,
the ruler ordered that the artisan
be brought before him.

At the appointed hour on the appointed day, the visitor was ushered into the rose garden, where the sultan was reclining on a splendid divan.

‘I shall make for you a clock with many faces, Your Magnificence,’ the clockmaker said obsequiously. ‘I will design it to show the time in every realm, with the hemispheres and the planets as well – each of them revolving around Your Excellency’s own indomitable shadow.’

The sultan touched a hand to his chin. Grovelling pleased him, and so he did not speak until he was sure there was no more fawning to come.

Then he said:
'I have an entire wing of the palace filled with clocks! I have big clocks and small clocks, clocks fashioned from gold and silver, from precious gems and the rarest wood.

'I have clocks that chime and others that play dainty tunes. I have clocks that open up to reveal yet more clocks, and I have clocks that tell the time in ways you yourself have surely never imagined possible!'

The clockmaker glanced down at the gravel beneath his feet. He didn't want to say it, but it seemed as though the sultan had enough clocks already.

Just as he was about to say something suitably ingratiating, the ruler beckoned him closer. Apprehensively, the artisan approached the royal divan.

‘I do not want a clock,’ said the sultan.
‘Ah,’ intoned the clockmaker.
‘No, no,’ the sultan said. ‘Not a clock…
but a *chair*. I want a chair instead.’

The clockmaker frowned.
'Then I shall find a great carpenter,
Your Magnificence,' he whispered.

The sultan held up a finger.
'A chair,' he went on, 'that is powered by clockwork, and that can travel through time.'

Still frowning, the clockmaker blinked.
'Travel through *what*...?'
'*Time*. A chair that can travel through time.'
'But... but... but, Your Magnificence,'
the artisan squirmed.

The sultan brushed a hand through the air. 'Fail me,' he said, almost as an afterthought, 'and every member of your family shall be hunted out and slain, and their bones ground down to dust!'

The next thing the clockmaker knew, he was in his workshop with a royal command… and with a problem the size of the sultan's ego itself.

'How will I ever make a clockwork chair that can travel through time?' he moaned. 'I have a single month to complete the task. Disappoint the sultan and he'll swipe off my head, and that's just the start.'

The clockmaker's assistant sighed.
'The only way to accomplish this feat is to
enlist the help of a jinn,' he whispered.

‘What nonsense are you uttering?’
‘The soul of a jinn,’ the assistant explained.
‘You will need to trap a jinn and
harness his soul.’

'Whatever for?'

'Well,' said his assistant, 'as everyone knows full well, jinns can travel through the firmament, vaulting from one sphere to the next.'

‘A clockwork chair powered
by means of a jinn?’

The assistant sniffed.
'Indeed, master.'

'But how would I ever get my hands
on a jinn?'
'With a trap.'
'And how, pray tell, would I trap a jinn?'
'With a narwhal's tusk, of course.'

There were many things unknown and misunderstood at the time in which the clockmaker lived. But none of them, thankfully, was the business of trapping a jinn using a narwhal's tusk.

An hour or two in the magicians' market, and the clockmaker had all the equipment necessary to catch himself a jinn and to enslave it to his cause.

Turning on his heel, he set off into the desert, where the jinns liked to spend their nights sprawled out on the cool, empty sands.

In one hand he had a basket of finely chopped green chillies, and in the other, a bowl of camphor. Strapped to his back was a narwhal's tusk, the long, twisting strand of ivory catching the last strains of evening sunlight.

A few miles from town,
the clockmaker set up a camp.

Collecting a little firewood and dried palm fronds, he lit a fire and threw the camphor onto the flames.

A cloud of pungent smoke billowed out over the desiccated sands, dissipating into the night. The clockmaker waited, as he had been instructed to do by the jinn-catching expert in the magicians' bazaar.

He waited and waited,
and eventually fell asleep.

Moments after dawn, as he made up his mind to return home, he heard a rattling sound. It grew louder and louder, until it seemed as though each grain of sand for a thousand miles was shaking.

Boom! Boom! Boom!

The clockmaker feared an invading army was marching towards him.

Raising a hand to his brow,
he scanned the horizon.
Nothing.

But the booming went on,
the desert shuddering.

Peering with all his might, the clockmaker spied a dust cloud far away. It was heading towards him. Again, he scanned the distance, squinting into the blinding light.

Eventually, he saw it.
Or, rather, he glimpsed something…

A pair of feet as big as boulders, gunmetal grey
and moving fitfully one after the other.

Above them were the legs and the body,
the arms and the head. Colossal, unyielding,
imposing in the most debased of ways.

The clockmaker would have run,
but his gut told him to hold fast. Terrified,
he waited until the immense figure was
looming over him. One more step and
he would have been crushed.

The creature, a jinn called Mezmiss,
stopped an inch away.

Its shadow fell upon him – freezing and dark,
it stank of death and destruction.
'Who dares summon me, Mezmiss,
Master of all Jinns?' cried the monster.

The clockmaker stepped back,
hoping to escape the fearful shadow.
But, as soon as he broke free from the shade,
he caught sight of the jinn's features –
and wished he had never seen them at all.

‘I am a clockmaker, Your Jinnship,’ he said. ‘And it was I who called you to meet me in this place.’

The monster grunted.
'By whose authority did you dare
to summon me?'

‘On the authority of the ivory king!’
the clockmaker stammered,
his neck craning back.
‘Then where is his sword, thou feeble human?’

Holding the narwhal's tusk above his head, the clockmaker gritted his teeth and snarled as he had been told to do.

The ground shook as never before as the jinn, Mezmiss, collapsed to his knees.

Without wasting a moment, the clockmaker ran forwards and threw the chillies into the monster's eyes.

As the creature was floundering in pain,
the clockmaker climbed onto its head and
dug his thumbs into its nostrils.
'I am your master now!' he declared.
'I and only I!'

Mezmiss lowered his head in subservience. 'So be it,' he uttered reticently. 'What is your wish, O human?'

Climbing down, the clockmaker held the ivory tusk out before him. 'My wish is for you to travel to another time, and to take me with you.'

The Master of all Jinns snarled his most diabolical snarl, enraged that the mortal knew of the secret formula to harness a jinn's inner strength.

Reciting an incantation as he burned another block of camphor, the clockmaker wore the monster down until he was no more than a grey, fleshy lump of pulp.

‘So be it,’ whimpered the jinn, his menacing tone now gone, ‘I will lend you my soul, so long as you promise to return it.’

The clockmaker made a solemn guarantee
and, before he knew it, a hoopoe was
singing before him in a cage.
'There it is,' said the jinn, his strength
all spent. 'There is my soul.'

Leaving the desert, the clockmaker hastened back to his workshop, where he hung the cage on a hook and got to work. He devised an interlocking gearing system, using hydraulics and dials, astrolabes and cogs – a mechanism that would harness the power of the jinn's soul.

The only thing on the craftsman's mind was preserving his throat.

On the morning of the deadline, the sultan sat perched on his throne waiting for the clockmaker to arrive, fingertips pressed together in contemplation.

'Perhaps he has fled, Majesty,'
said the chief minister.
'Or has taken his own life,'
another courtier taunted.

The sultan glanced at his favourite clock as it struck the midday hour.

At that moment, there was the sound of iron wheels moving over wood.

The clockmaker stepped cautiously into the throne room. He was holding a square cage in which the hoopoe was chirping. Behind him was wheeled a large mechanical device covered in a silky cloth.

The sultan craned forwards,
squinting to focus on the bird.
'What is a hoopoe doing here?!' he bellowed.

The artisan smiled demurely.

'It is more than a mere bird,' he said. 'It is the soul of a jinn, a jinn who can travel back and forwards in time.'

Jerking away the cloth,
the clockmaker revealed his creation.

Elaborate in every way, the intricate and interwoven mechanism was encased in glass, so that every moving part could be clearly seen and admired.

At the front, upholstered in crushed vermilion velvet, was a grand fauteuil. The clockmaker opened a door in the contraption, slotted the bird's cage into position, and bowed reverently.

As he did so, the machine came to life.

The dials began to revolve, the cogs rotate,
and the astrolabes flash as they caught light
from the crystal chandelier above.

In the middle of it all, alarmed
by the mechanism around it,
the little hoopoe tweeted fitfully.

'It is ready, Your Majesty,'
said the clockmaker, a tone of anxiety
in his voice, for he had not yet had the time
to test his machine.

The sultan got to his feet and stepped over.
'Are you certain that it works?'

The craftsman looked at him hard,
their eyes locked onto each other.
'Indeed, Your Majesty,' he said.

The sultan narrowed his eyes as if
brooding on an idea.
'Go back to the tenth year in the
reign of the Caliph Harun ar-Rachid,
to the great citadel of Baghdad, and bring
me the imperial signet ring.'

The clockmaker took a step backwards.
He touched a finger to his Adam's apple,
at the point where he imagined the
executioner's blade would fall.

'A great challenge, Your Majesty,'
he said coldly.
The sultan smiled at the corner of his mouth.
'Off you go, then,' he said.

With a deep sigh, the clockmaker stepped up into the chair, the hoopoe still tweeting against the sound of the mechanism. Adjusting the dials, he checked the pressure on a pair of gauges, then pressed a button in the middle of the instrument panel.

With the bird chirping in terror, the machine shuddered and spluttered to breaking point.

Then, it vanished.

The sultan's eyes widened;
he was too shocked to speak.

Where the machine had so recently stood was a patch of slimy blue oil.

The sultan inspected it from a distance.
'How dare he sully the royal court,' he said.

Clinging to the velvet seat, the clockmaker's corporal form was displaced across time and reconstituted as it reached the tenth year of Harun ar-Rachid's reign.

The first sound to touch
his ears was the little hoopoe.
He smiled.
'Thank God it's still alive,' he said.

The clockmaker was about to step out of the chair when a party of imperial soldiers marched up, grabbed him, and trussed him in chains. As for the machine, it was loaded onto a cart and taken away, the hoopoe chirping wildly in fright.

As the city of Baghdad slept below, the prisoner was taken to a tower in the citadel with a view out over the Tigris. Beaten and bruised, he was hung up on a cell's wall, a bucket of animal blood hurled over him for good measure.

The jailer, who doubled as a torturer and sometimes executioner as well, held up a pair of pliers and grinned a toothless grin. He was a vile and putrid example of manhood, one who derived pleasure from wielding authority.

Preparing himself for torture, the clockmaker said a prayer to the Master of All Jinns.

As he did so, the jailer stepped forward, his pliers splayed apart and ready for use. ‘Open your mouth,’ he grunted, ‘and we’ll get down to work.’

At that moment, there was the sound
of leather boots rasping on stone.

An officer from the royal guard had climbed the steps to the tower and was racing down through the cell block.

Banging on the reinforced iron door,
he ordered the jailer to open up.
'Get him down at once!' the officer shouted.
'I have orders to take the prisoner!'

The jailer's face fell.
Lowering his trusty tool, he asked:
'And who might have signed these orders?'

‘The Caliph Harun ar-Rachid himself!’

The clockmaker was unchained, and the next thing he knew, he was in the throne room on his knees. Reclining on a voluminous gilded throne before him was the Caliph Harun of *A Thousand and One Nights*.

Sweeping through the chamber, a vizier whispered in his master's ear before melting away into the shadows. Narrowing his eyes, the caliph remained silent for a long while.

Eventually, in a slow and deliberate voice,
he spoke:
'I have come to understand that you were
discovered with a mechanical device.'

The caliph touched the arm of his throne in a signal. A curtain was lowered at the far end of the hall, revealing the clockmaker's chair.

His eyes fixed in terror to the floor, its inventor cocked his head up and down in affirmation. So fearful was he that he dared not look up at the caliph's hands to check them for the imperial signet ring.

'Your Magnificence,' he babbled, his voice barely audible. 'Yes, I created the machine.'

'And what purpose does it serve?'

The artisan said nothing, terrified of being executed on the spot as a sorcerer.

The caliph, Master of the Known Universe, repeated his question, a strain of displeasure in his voice.

‘It… it… it…’ started the clockmaker, ‘is a contrivancc by which the spheres of the cosmos may be breached by the frailties of man.’

Smoothing down an eyebrow with the tip of his index finger, the caliph walked over to the machine and inspected it studiously. His attentive gaze took in the dials and the levers, the gauges and the gears.

‘And what provides propulsion?’ he asked.
‘A little hoopoe, Your Majesty,’
said the clockmaker.
‘A simple bird?’
The caliph broke into a smile.

'A bird, Your Highness,' repeated the clockmaker, 'but not a *simple* bird.'
'And where is it, this bird?'

Getting to his feet, the clockmaker paced over to his machine and leant down to where the cage had been placed. His expression went from one of fear to one of extreme alarm.

‘The hoopoe has gone!’ he cried.

Unable to witness a demonstration of the device, the caliph clapped his hands and the clockmaker was taken away back to the cells.

As for the machine, it was dragged
to the stables and left to rust.

Now, it so happened that one of the guards entrusted with the job of hauling the machine to the caliph's throne room had heard the hoopoe chirping.

Taking pity on the little creature, he removed its cage and took the bird home, where he fed it some choice morsels of meat.

The next morning, the guard's daughter woke before her father and, finding the bird there, she jumped up and down with delight. Eager to pick it up and caress its delicate plumage, she opened the cage door.

Instantly, the hoopoe flew from the cage and out of the open window.

Locked up in the tower, the clockmaker damned himself for his reverse in fortune, and he cursed the person who had taken the soul of Mezmiss, Master of All Jinns. He was certain that any minute now the jailer would be along to wrench out his teeth.

The hoopoe flapped its way over Baghdad, the city of gardens, palaces, and fountains. Unable to believe its luck at being set free at last and to have been transported to such luxuriant surroundings, the bird flew down to a large garden and began pecking the lawn for worms.

By chance, the garden belonged to a royal princess, the daughter of the caliph himself. Her name was Princess Amina, and she loved nothing more than little hoopoes.

Sitting in the shade of her balcony, she spied the bird foraging about and she gave the order for her gardener to fetch the creature and to put it in a cage.

Within an hour, the bird had been trapped in an unwieldy butterfly net and was hanging in a gilded cage in the princess's bedroom. That night, the hoopoe serenaded its new owner to sleep.

As she slept, the princess had the most remarkable dream of her life.

She dreamed that a stranger arrived from another time and took her on a fabulous machine to a land where rainbow waterfalls cascaded down from the sky.

And she dreamed that this stranger was the most talented and kind man in existence, but that he was languishing at that very moment in the most gruesome of cells – lost somewhere in her father's prison.

The next morning, the princess awoke to the sound of the hoopoe singing once again. Her eyes wide with wonder, she sat bolt upright and called for her lady-in-waiting.

'You must hurry to the cells,' she said, 'and search out a foreigner who is being tortured there.'
'But how will I know him, Your Highness?'

The princess thought for a moment. 'Take the hoopoe,' she replied, 'and when he sings, you would have found the prisoner I want to see. Bring them both to me – and waste not a moment!'

Just as the torturer was once again peering into the clockmaker's mouth, there came the dainty sound of a woman's voice at the door of the cell. Grimacing, the jailer slid back the bolts to find the princess's lady-in-waiting, a caged bird in her hand.

No sooner had the hoopoe's tiny eye
spotted the artisan than the bird began
to sing rapturously.

'That's him!' exclaimed the princess's attendant. 'Release him. Princess Amina is awaiting him this very moment!' With a sigh, the jailer unlocked the chains a second time.

Filthy, bleeding, and reeking of fear, the clockmaker was brought to the princess's private salon. He stood in the doorway, his shoulders hunched low, while the hoopoe's cage was hung near to the window.

It wasn't long before the princess
stepped in from the garden.

The clockmaker found himself unable to speak, having never before been in the presence of such beauty. The princess was silent too, her heart warmed by the stranger's gentle sensitivity.

'Last night, I had a dream,' she began, explaining why she had called the clockmaker to her private apartment.

The couple spent the afternoon together in conversation and laughter. They felt drawn to each other, as if nothing in the world could keep them apart.

Suddenly, the clockmaker put a
hand to his mouth in fear.
'How will I ever get back to my mechanism?'
he asked despondently.

Leaning forwards, Princess Amina
brushed a hand over his cheek.
'I shall help you,' she said.

Word had swept through the
palace that one of the convicts had
been invited to the princess's private
apartment, the news eventually reaching
the ears of the caliph himself.

Enraged that his favourite daughter should be fraternizing with a common prisoner, Harun ar-Rachid ordered for the machine, the hoopoe, the clockmaker, and Princess Amina to be brought before him at once.

Setting eyes on his time-travelling chair,
the clockmaker's heart beat all the faster.
The bird, the mechanism, and the caliph's
imperial signet ring were all in the same room.

But there were armed guards at every door. One wrong move and he would breathe his last.

‘If Your Majesty should like a demonstration of the machine,’ said the artisan, plucking up courage to speak, ‘I would happily oblige.’

The caliph signalled to the guard for the prisoner's chains to be unfastened. 'Try and escape,' he said, 'and you will be hacked down before you can touch a finger to your nose.'

The perspiration beading into droplets on his brow, the clockmaker picked up the hoopoe's cage and fixed it into position.

‘With the bird installed, Your Majesty,’
he said, ‘the contrivance is ready for use.
The administrator sits in the chair like this,
and arranges the instruments like so.
And then…’

Before he could finish his sentence,
the clockmaker, the hoopoe, and the machine
disappeared – leaving the caliph, his daughter,
and the guards in astonished silence.

Anyone with sharp eyes may have noticed that the ring on Harun's finger had vanished as well.

A moment after that, there was a thundering commotion and the mechanism reappeared in plain sight.

The clockmaker was still seated calmly on the velvet-covered chair. On his finger was the imperial signet ring of Harun ar-Rachid.

A band of gold, mined in the bleak caves of Nubia, it was said to possess power over the heavens and the earth.

In one movement, the artisan reached forward, took the hand of the princess, and invited her to sit beside him. She did so and, instantly, the machine vanished once again.

Back in his own time, the travelling clockmaker kept his promise. Releasing the hoopoe, he gave the jinn freedom and returned him back to himself.

Then, summoning the power of the imperial signet ring, he had the sultan and his courtiers turned into parrots, which flapped up into the trees.

Finally, he proposed to Amina, the favourite
daughter of Caliph Harun ar-Rachid.
The princess accepted.

When the couple had been wed,
they continued on their journeys.

Without the need for time-travelling machines, imperial signet rings, or jinns, they set off on foot one night, their gaze trained up at the stars.

Finis

About the Author

Descended from a long line of storytellers, writers, and savants, Tahir Shah is one of the most prolific authors of his generation. He has published more than sixty books in numerous genres, including travel, fiction, and fantasy, as well as tales for children.

Raised in the tradition of Eastern 'teaching stories', Shah is passionate about stories and storytelling. He regards the ability to learn from folklore as being in us all, what he calls a 'default setting of humankind'. As well as having written scores of books, Shah has made documentaries for National Geographic TV and The History Channel. He is the founder and CEO of the charity, The Scheherazade Foundation.

About the Artist

Anca Chelaru grew up in a small town in Romania, where she picked up a passion for art and stories from her family's extensive library. She studied at the Ion Mincu University of Architecture and Urban Planning in Bucharest, and soon began pursuing her interest in book illustration – with a particular interest in fantasy and the surreal. Her main sources of artistic inspiration are the art nouveau movement and the post-war Romanian illustrators.

Books By Tahir Shah

The Writer's Craft

The Reason to Write

Workbook: Comprehensive, Volume I & II

Workbook: Fantasy, Volume I & II

Workbook: Fiction, Volume I & II

Workbook: Historical Fiction, Volume I & II

Workbook: Teaching Stories, Volume I & II

Workbook: Travel, Volume I & II

Novels

Jinn Hunter: Book One – The Prism

Jinn Hunter: Book Two – The Jinnslayer

Jinn Hunter: Book Three – The Perplexity

Hannibal Fogg and the Supreme Secret of Man

Casablanca Blues

Eye Spy

Godman

Paris Syndrome

Timbuctoo

Midas

Zigzagzone

Nasrudin

Travels With Nasrudin

The Misadventures of the Mystifying Nasrudin

The Peregrinations of the Perplexing Nasrudin

The Voyages and Vicissitudes of Nasrudin

Nasrudin in the Land of Fools

Travel

Trail of Feathers
Travels With Myself
Beyond the Devil's Teeth
In Search of King Solomon's Mines
House of the Tiger King
In Arabian Nights
The Caliph's House
Sorcerer's Apprentice
Journey Through Namibia

Teaching Stories

The Arabian Nights Adventures
Scorpion Soup
Tales Told to a Melon
The Afghan Notebook
Daydreams of an Octopus & Other Stories
The Caravanserai Stories
Ghoul Brothers
Hourglass
Imaginist
Jinn's Treasure
Jinnlore
Mellified Man
Skeleton Island
Wellspring
When the Sun Forgot to Rise
Outrunning the Reaper
The Cap of Invisibility
On Backgammon Time
The Wondrous Seed

The Paradise Tree
Mouse House
The Hoopoe's Flight
The Old Wind
A Treasury of Tales
The Tale of Double Six
The Forgotten Game
King of the Jinns
The Destiny Ring
Changing the World
Cat, Mouse
Frogland
Mittle-Mittle
Capilongo
The Princess of Zilzilam
The Singing Serpents
The Tale of the Rusty Nail
The Unicorn's Tear
The Clockmaker Who Travelled Through Time
The Fish's Dream
The Man Whose Arms Grew Branches
The Most Foolish of Men
The Shop That Sold Truth
Qwerty
Renaissance
The Man With the Tiger's Head
The Kingdom of Blink
The Wisdom of Celestine
Dream Soup
The Skeleton Factory
An Unexpected Gift

The Problem Exchange
The Pharaoh Code
The Monkey Puzzle Club
Liquid Time
Cat Dog, Dog Cat
Princess Pickle's Laugh

Anthologies
The Anthologies: Africa
The Anthologies: Ceremony
The Anthologies: Childhood
The Anthologies: City
The Anthologies: Danger
The Anthologies: East
The Anthologies: Expedition
The Anthologies: Frontier
The Anthologies: Hinterland
The Anthologies: India
The Anthologies: Jinns
The Anthologies: Jungle
The Anthologies: Magic
The Anthologies: Morocco
The Anthologies: Nasrudin
The Anthologies: People
The Anthologies: Quest
The Anthologies: South
The Anthologies: Taboo
The Anthologies: Teaching Stories
The Clockmaker's Box
The Tahir Shah Fiction Reader
The Tahir Shah Travel Reader

Research

Cultural Research

The Middle East Bedside Book

Three Essays

Edited by

Congress With a Crocodile

A Son of a Son, Volume I

A Son of a Son, Volume II

Screenplays

Casablanca Blues: The Screenplay

Timbuctoo: The Screenplay

A REQUEST

If you enjoyed this book, please review it on your favourite online retailer or review website.

Reviews are an author's best friend.

To stay in touch with Tahir Shah, and to hear about his upcoming releases before anyone else, please sign up for his mailing list:

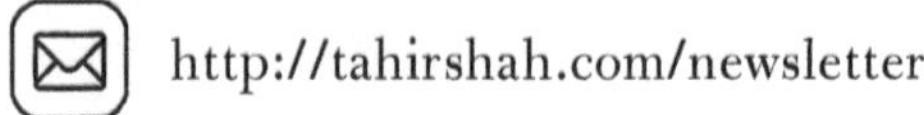
http://tahirshah.com/newsletter

And to follow him on social media, please go to any of the following links:

http://www.twitter.com/humanstew

@tahirshah999

http://www.facebook.com/TahirShahAuthor

http://www.youtube.com/user/tahirshah999

http://www.pinterest.com/tahirshah

https://www.goodreads.com/tahirshahauthor

http://www.tahirshah.com

www.ingramcontent.com/pod-product-compliance
Lightning Source LLC
Chambersburg PA
CBHW030521310726
48979CB00010B/1750/J

* 9 7 8 1 9 1 5 8 7 6 0 9 6 *